For Eleanor Grace, with love from Jamma — JMS

To Aunty Ivy — YLK

Tundra Books, an imprint of Tundra Book Group, a division of Penguin Random House of Canada Limited

Library and Archives Canada Cataloguing in Publication

Title: The care and keeping of grandmas / Jennifer Mook-Sang ; illustrated by Yong Ling Kang.
Names: Mook-Sang, Jennifer, author. | Kang, Yong Ling, illustrator.
Identifiers: Canadiana (print) 20220177724 | Canadiana (ebook) 20220177732 |
ISBN 9780735271340 (hardcover) | ISBN 9780735271357 (EPUB)
Classification: LCC PS8626.O59264 C38 2023 | DDC jC813/.6—dc23

Published simultaneously in the United States of America by Tundra Books of Northern New York, an imprint of Tundra Book Group, a division of Penguin Random House of Canada Limited

Library of Congress Control Number: 2022933332

Edited by Samantha Swenson
Designed by John Martz
The artwork in this book was created with watercolor and pencil.
The text was set in Stratford.

Printed in China

www.penguinrandomhouse.ca

1   2   3   4   5   27   26   25   24   23

Penguin
Random House
tundra | TUNDRA BOOKS

The CARE and KEEPING of Grandmas

WRITTEN BY Jennifer Mook-Sang

ILLUSTRATED BY Yong Ling Kang

tundra

In their usual habitats, you might find grandmas baking, gardening, rug hooking, parasailing and bungee jumping.

Their homes could be just like yours, or they might be in trees, on rivers, in campers or on hillsides.

One day, your grandma may leave her home — for yours!

When my grandma came to live with us, she had to get used to a new environment.

I tried my best to make
her comfortable.

I showed her around and introduced her to our pets
and neighbors and other family members.

I helped her create a personal space that was all hers,
and we decorated it with her favorite things.

I kept her company whenever
she needed some quiet time.

I made sure she had lots of light, especially in the morning when the sun shines in.

My grandma was discombobulated by changes to her routine. But I was patient.

Eventually,
we found plans that
worked for everyone.

I fed my grandma regularly.

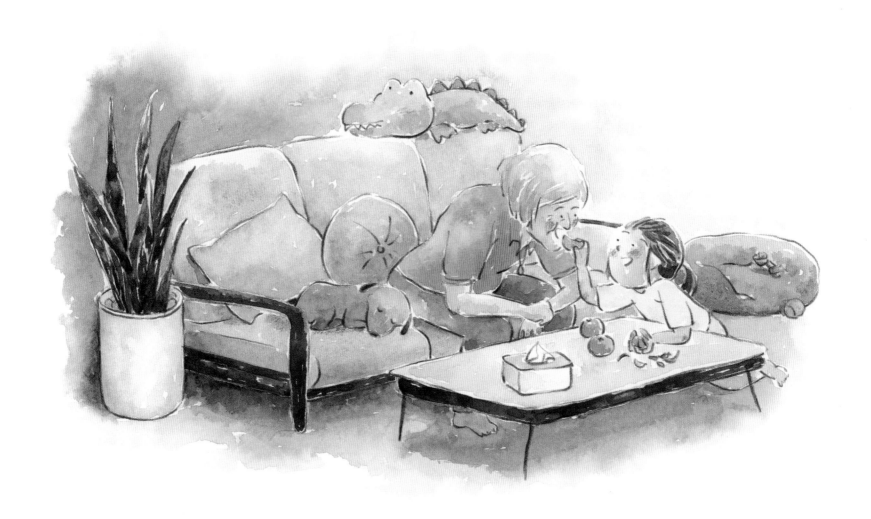

I kept her well-watered.

And I tidied her up when she needed it!

Grandmas can't do
everything themselves,

so I was always there
when she needed me.

Even with all my help, though, my grandma was sometimes a little wilted.

In those moments,
I knew just what to do.

It took some time for my grandma to settle in
and really feel at home. But now, it's
like she has always been here.